Uncle Gus's
Magic Box

By Ted van Lieshout
Illustrations by Philip Hopman
Translated by Simona Sideri

Uncle Gus's Magic Box

ANNICK PRESS

TORONTO + NEW YORK + VANCOUVER

Text © 2005 Ted van Lieshout
Illustrations © 2005 Philip Hopman
Translation © 2005 Simona Sideri

Annick Press Ltd.
First published by Van Goor, Amsterdam under the title *Goochelaar!*

We acknowledge the support of the Canada Council for the Arts, the Ontario
Arts Council, and the Government of Canada through the Book Publishing Industry
Development Program (BPIDP) for our publishing activities.

Copy edited by Elizabeth McLean
Cover and interior design by Irvin Cheung/iCheung Design

The text was typeset in The Sans

Cataloging in Publication
Lieshout, Ted van
Uncle Gus's magic box / Ted van Lieshout ; illustrations
by Philip Hopman ; translated by Simona Sideri. — North American ed.

Translation of: Goochelaar!
ISBN 1-55037-935-6 (bound).—ISBN 1-55037-934-8 (pbk.)

I. Hopman, Philip II. Sideri, Simona III. Title.

PZ7.L64Un 2005   j839.31'364   C2005-900904-7

Printed and bound in Canada

Published in the U.S.A. by	**Distributed in Canada by:**	**Distributed in the U.S.A. by:**
Annick Press (U.S.) Ltd.	Firefly Books Ltd.	Firefly Books (U.S.) Inc.
	66 Leek Crescent	P.O. Box 1338
	Richmond Hill, ON	Ellicott Station
	L4B 1H1	Buffalo, NY 14205

Visit our website at: **www.annickpress.com**

Spoof ran to the door.
He wagged his tail.
He barked.
He was happy because Dad was home.
Dad walked in.
He was hungry.
"Give me three cookies,"
he said. "Or I'll die."
I gave him one.

"Three is too many," I said.
I ate the second cookie.
Spoof got half of the third one and
I ate the rest of it.

Dad sat on the couch.
He looked through the mail.
"There's a letter for you," he said.

"For me?" I asked, surprised.
I never get any mail,
except on my birthday.
But it wasn't my birthday.

I took the letter.
It had my name on it.
I opened it quickly.
It said:

`Your long-lost uncle is dead.`

"My long-lost uncle is dead,"
I told Dad.

"Your long-lost uncle?
That must be Uncle Gus.
You haven't got any other long-lost uncles."

"I don't know Uncle Gus," I said.

"Uncle Gus only saw you once,"
said Dad. "You were still in your crib.
Then he moved to Japan."

"Because of me?" I asked.

"Probably," laughed Dad.
"What does the letter say?"

I read it out:

"Sadly, your long-lost uncle has died.
But the good news is that he left you
something.
It's on its way, by mail."

"How exciting!" exclaimed Dad.
"What else does the letter say?
Anything about me?
Has he left me something?"

I shook my head.
"It doesn't say anything else," I said.
"Just, Respectfully."

Dad looked through the rest of the mail.
He wanted to be left something by Uncle Gus, too.
But no, there was no letter for him.

The doorbell rang.
I ran to see who it was.
The mailman was standing on the porch.

He was carrying a large package.
It was too heavy for me.
Dad came to help.
He dragged the package inside.

There was a letter with it.
It said:

Your long-lost uncle left you this.
Enjoy it.
Respectfully.

I tore off the wrapping.
Inside was a box.
I wanted to open the lid
but the box was locked and
the key was nowhere to be found.

"I know!" shouted Dad.
He ran to the shed.
He came back with his toolbox.
He hit the lock with a wrench.
He poked it with a screwdriver.
He loosened a screw
and then tightened it again.
He sawed a piece off the lock.
He filed and hammered for half an hour.
But the box stayed locked tight.
I was disappointed.

"Look in the letter again,"
panted Dad, tired out from his hard work.
"There must be a key somewhere.
Look in the envelope."

I looked inside.
"Hooray!" I yelled. "Here it is.
I just didn't notice it!"

"For crying out loud," said Dad.
He fell back onto the couch.
"Couldn't you have checked there first?"

I stuck the key in the lock.
Then I turned it.
The lock creaked a bit.
The lid opened.
I saw lots of strange things inside the box:
a black hat, a bow tie.
I also saw a little stick...

"Dad, was my long-lost uncle a magician?"

"Yes, that's right," said Dad.
"How did you know?"

"Well, this is a magician's wand.
I think he's left me a magician's box."

"That's nice," said Dad.
"If you practice, you can become a magician, too."

"That would be a good job," I said.
I looked in the box for a book
to teach me how to do tricks.

Nothing. There was no book.
"How can I become a good magician
if I don't know how to do magic?"

"That's for you to figure out," said Dad.
"Uncle Gus left you that box.
He didn't leave me anything.
Nothing. Not even a cent."

I put the black hat on.
It was too big, but that was okay.
I tied the bow tie round my neck.
I waved the wand.
Nothing happened.
I took the hat off and looked inside.
There was no rabbit in it.
There was no dove.
There wasn't even a bunch of flowers.

I tapped the wand against the brim.
I looked in the hat again.
There was nothing to be seen.
I said solemnly,
"Simsalabim!...
Hocus pocus!...
Abracadabra!..."
Nothing happened.

"You know what I think, Dad?
I'm still wearing my old jeans and shirt.
That's why it's not working.
Can you buy me a magician's outfit?"

"No way," said Dad.
"Don't even think about it.
Your long-lost uncle didn't leave me anything.
So I haven't got any money for a magician's outfit."

I looked in the box again.
Maybe the book was in the bottom.
I pushed the box over on its side.
Everything fell out.
Then I pulled the box upright again.
Aha! A piece of paper was stuck to the bottom.
There was something written on it:

How to cut an orphan girl in half

Lie an orphan girl in the box.
Close the lid.
Take the saw.
Saw the box in half.
The orphan girl is sawn in half.
Show the audience the two halves.
Put the two halves together again.
Open the lid.
The orphan girl steps out of the box.
She is whole again!

"Dad, I need an orphan girl."

"An orphan girl?" asked Dad.
"Where are you going to get an orphan girl from?
I don't know any orphan girls.
I only know one orphan.
That's me.
My parents are dead."

"Oh, well," I said.
"It will probably work just as well with an orphan dad.
Dad, can you get in the box?"

"And then?" asked Dad.

"Then I'm going to saw you in half."

"You must be joking," shouted Dad.
"That will hurt too much!"

"It won't hurt," I said.
"Because it's a magic trick."

"All right, then," said Dad.

Dad got in the box.
Spoof was the audience.
He wagged his tail from side to side.
He thought it was very exciting.
I closed the lid.
Dad's head stuck out of one end of the box.
His feet stuck out the other end.
I grabbed the saw.
I cleared my throat and said gravely,
"Distinkished members of the audience!"

"That's not right," said Dad.
"It's '*Distinguished* members
of the audience!'"

"Okay.
Distinguished members of the audience!"
Spoof wagged his tail faster.
"Now... I am going to saw an orphan dad in half!"

I started to saw.

The box had to be sawn in half.

Dad hollered.

He gasped for breath and said,
"I don't like to complain, but this feels weird!"

"Don't worry," I panted.

It was hard work. But I did it.

I pushed the two halves of the box apart.

I showed Spoof that it was real.

The dog didn't understand what was going on.

He whimpered a bit.

Then I pushed the two halves together again.

I lifted the lid.

"Ta daaaa!" I shouted proudly.

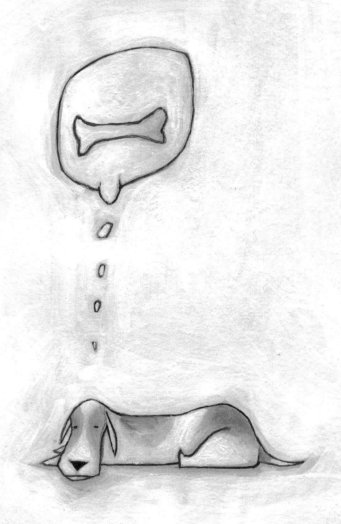

But Dad didn't stand up.

He didn't step out of the box.

"Dad!" I hissed.

"Come out, now!"

"I... I..." mumbled Dad.

"I can't!"

"Don't be silly, Dad.

The audience will leave."

Spoof was looking to the left.

He was looking to the right.

He was looking to the back.

But he wasn't looking at us anymore.

He thought it was boring.

He yawned as if he was thinking,

"If only I had a bone."

"Dad, come on!" I said crossly.
"Don't make a scene."

"I'm not making a scene," shouted Dad.
"I just can't get out!"

So I looked in the box.
I was shocked at what I saw.
The magic trick had gone wrong.
Dad was cut in half.
He lay there in two bits.
Luckily, he wasn't bleeding.

"Oh, Dad!" I cried.
"You really *are* sawn in half!"

Dad felt with his hands.
"What a dumb magic trick," he said.
"You're a terrible magician!"

"That's because..." I said,
"you didn't get me a magician's outfit."

"Nonsense!" said Dad.

"Well, then..." I said, "it's because
you're not an orphan girl."
I bit my lip.

"Does it hurt, Dad?"

"No," said Dad.
"Funnily, it doesn't hurt at all."

"Well," I said.
"The trick didn't go completely wrong!
Someone cut in half hurts.
You don't.
Someone cut in half bleeds a lot.
You don't.
So the trick is half right.
I'm half a magician.
That's what I think."

"What are you babbling about now?" said Dad.
"Do something! I miss my legs.
And my legs miss me.
Put me back together, you half a magician!"

I looked through all the stuff
from the magician's box.
There was nothing there.
"There are no more instructions," I said.
"There's just:
How to cut an orphan girl in half.
There's no note saying anything else.
You know what?
I'm going to call 911. They will know what to do."

"That's a good idea," said Dad.
"But first help me out of the box.
I'm tired of lying down."

I dragged Dad's bottom half out of the box.
I stood him up.

"And now me," said Dad's top half.
I pulled him out of the box.
"Now there are two of me," said Dad quietly.
He looked sadly at his bottom half.
He stroked his knee.
Spoof licked his other knee.

I called the emergency number.
"My dad is broken!" I shouted.

"What happened?" asked the woman who answered.

"I sawed him in half," I said.

"Why?" asked the woman.
"Was it to punish him?"

"Er... no," I said.

"Did you do it on purpose?
Because if you did, you need the police."

"No, it was an accident."

"We'll send help right away, then," said the woman.

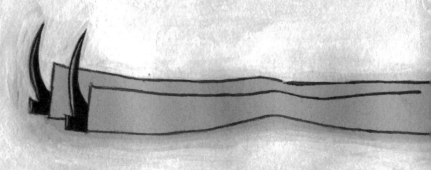

Then I quickly fetched some bandages.
They're useful when there's been an accident.
I rolled Dad onto the floor and stuck his two
halves together with bandages.
Dad had taught me that if someone's hurt
you give them first aid.
So that's what I did.

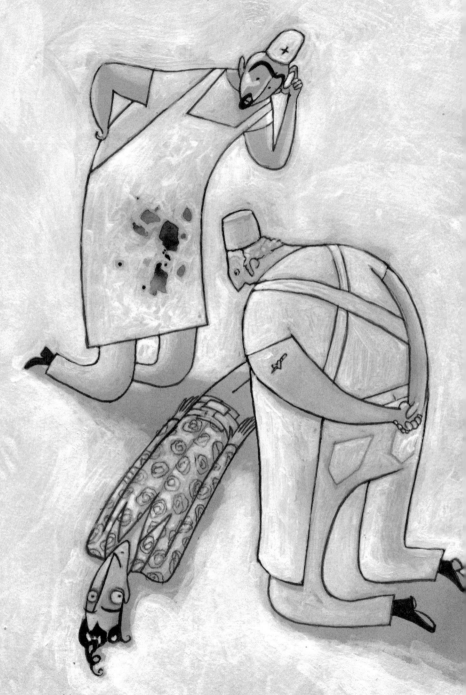

I heard the ambulance coming.
The nurses came in.
They knelt next to Dad.
"Does it hurt a lot?" they asked.

"Not really," said Dad.

"Are you sure?" asked one nurse.

"You're cut in half!" said the other one.

Dad said, "The trick went wrong."

"Only half wrong," I said.
"I want to be a magician.
So I sawed an orphan dad in half."

"There's nothing we can do,"
said the nurse.
"We don't know any doctors who know magic.
You'll have to call an expert.
Maybe a magician can help.
Goodbye!"
Then they went away.
They left Dad lying there.

"But... but...
My dad needs to be fixed," I called.
I was not happy.
Dad was in two halves.
Each piece was smaller than me.
That was no good.

"Get the phone book," said Dad.
I fetched it and gave it to him.
He started to flick through the book wildly.
He was looking for a magician.

"Woof," went Spoof.

"What's wrong, Spoof?" I asked
because woof can mean lots of things.

"Woof woof," barked Spoof.
That was dog for:
"Come here!"

I went to Spoof.
He picked something up from the floor and
held it in his mouth.
It was the saw.
Oh, no, it wasn't the saw.
Not the saw I had used to cut Dad in half.
Now I got it.
I had used the wrong saw!
Not the one from the magician's box
but the saw from Dad's toolbox.
How stupid!

I knew what I had to do.
"Hey, Dad..."

"Not now," snarled Dad.
"I'm on the phone."
I heard Dad say,
"Well, I think it's really silly
that you won't explain how the trick works!"
He banged down the phone.

"I've got a plan, Dad.
 I'm going to save you."

"You can't," said Dad.
"You're not a real magician."

"I'm half a magician," I said.
"Come on, do what I say, Dad."
 I helped Dad get back in the box.
 First his bottom half,
 then his top half.
 Then I shut the lid again.

"What are you doing?" asked Dad.
 I grabbed the good saw: the magic saw.

"I'm going to saw again," I said.

"What's the use of that?
 That won't help," said Dad.
 He took a deep breath and sighed.

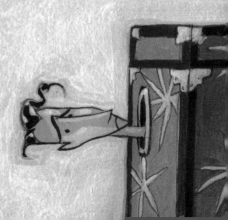

I sawed and sawed and sawed.
"Can you feel anything?" I asked.

"No," said Dad. "I can't feel anything."
I kept on sawing.

"Hee hee," said Dad,
"I feel tickling.
I feel tickling in my stomach."

Then I stopped sawing.
Slowly, I lifted the lid.
Had the trick worked?
Was Dad whole again?

Dad felt his body.
"I think..." said Dad.
"I think I'm in one piece again..."
Dad sat up.
He could do it by himself.
"You fixed me," cheered Dad.
"Hurray!"
He climbed out of the box.
He danced and jumped.
"What made you think of that?" asked Dad.
Spoof barked.

Luckily, Dad couldn't understand Spoof.
"I just thought of it," I said.

"That's so clever," cried Dad.
"You're a real magician!"

"That's right," I said.

"Help yourself to another cookie," said Dad.
I fetched the cookie jar and
took three cookies out.
One for Spoof.
One for me.
And another one for Spoof.

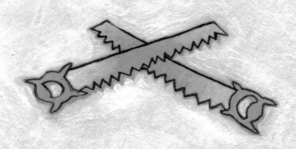